This Ladybird Book belongs to:

_____

_____

_____

_____

Retold by Liane B. Onish
Illustrated by Sally Long

Cover illustration by Thea Kliros

Copyright © Ladybird Books USA 1996

Originally published in the United Kingdom by Ladybird Books Ltd © 1993

First American edition by Ladybird Books USA
An Imprint of Penguin USA Inc.
375 Hudson Street, New York, New York 10014

Printed in Great Britain
10 9 8 7 6 5 4 3 2 1

ISBN 0-7214-5626-X

FAVORITE TALES

The Emperor's New Clothes

ong ago there lived a vain and foolish Emperor who loved clothes. He had clothes made of silk and satin, clothes made of the finest wools and trimmed with the softest furs, and even clothes spun with threads of pure gold. In fact, he had so many clothes he did not know what to wear.

One day, two clever men came to the palace to see the Emperor. "We are magic weavers," they said. "We can make a special, magic cloth that only the wise can see. When a fool looks at our cloth, he sees nothing at all."

The Emperor had never heard of such a wondrous cloth. Eagerly, he said, "Weavers, I command you to make me a suit out of your magical cloth."

The crafty weavers smiled at each other. "We shall need a great deal of gold thread," they said.

"You shall have all the thread you require," replied the Emperor.

The weavers filled their bags with gold thread and left the palace. They hid the gold and then sat at their looms and pretended to weave the magic cloth.

A week went by. The Emperor wondered how the weavers were doing.

"Prime Minister," he ordered, "See if my magic cloth is ready."

Clickety clack, clickety clack, the weavers were hard at work, but their looms were empty.

"Oh, dear," thought the Prime Minister. "I must be a fool! I see nothing on their looms. What shall I say to the Emperor?"

Afraid of being called a fool, the Prime Minister hurried off to tell the Emperor that the magic cloth was beautiful.

When the Prime Minister had gone, the weavers laughed and laughed. "What a fool!" they said.

"To sew the cloth into a suit, we need more gold thread," the weavers announced. They took the gold thread and hid it as before.

At last they brought the new suit to the palace.

The Emperor took off his clothes and the sly weavers fussed all around him.

"A perfect fit!" they cried.

The Emperor looked in the mirror but did not see any new suit at all. He did not want to seem foolish so he said, "It is beautiful."

"Magnificent!" said the weavers.

When the weavers left the palace, they burst out laughing.

"How clever we are," said one.

"And how silly and foolish the Emperor is!" laughed the other.

By now, everyone in the land had heard about the magic cloth and wanted to see it for themselves.

Soon messengers were sent out with a royal proclamation:

"Hear ye! Hear ye!
The Emperor will lead a grand
parade wearing his new clothes!"

When the great day arrived, the Emperor sent for the weavers to help him get dressed.

"Your Highness looks splendid!" they cried when they had finished. But still the Emperor could not see the new clothes.

The Emperor thought, "My Prime
Minister can see my new clothes. I cannot
be more foolish then he." So the Emperor
thanked the weavers and paid them
handsomely.

The trumpets blew and the grand procession began with the Emperor leading the way. People had come from far and near to see the Emperor in his new clothes.

When the crowd saw the Emperor in his new clothes, they were too stunned to speak. At last, a voice said timidly, "The Emperor's new clothes are beautiful!"

Then everyone started talking at once. "So fashionable!" "Very smart!" "Magnificent!" they said, each of them anxious not to seem more foolish than the next.

Then one small boy laughed out loud and exclaimed, "Look! The Emperor has no clothes on!"

Then *everyone* began to laugh.

"Oh no!" gasped the Emperor, turning red with embarrassment. "I have been the most foolish of all!"

As for the weavers, they were nowhere to
be seen!

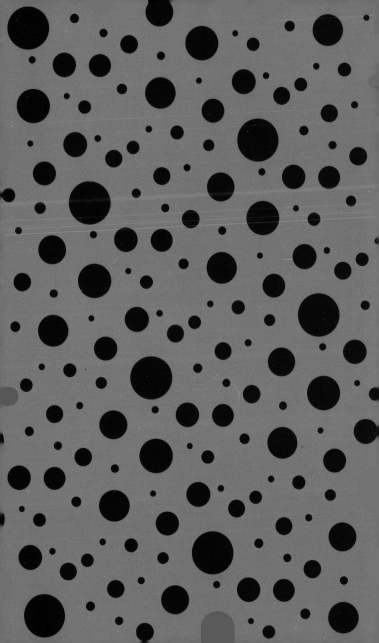